Tara The Dolphin

Written and Illustrated By

Shreya Kumar Pradhan

Dedication:

To the world's animals, especially dolphins and to the protection of the environment.

Thank you to my mom for inspiring me to write this story, and helping me assemble and publish this book.

ISBN: 9798449636287

Printed in the U.S.A.

There was a bottlenose dolphin named Tara, who had magical powers from accidentally touching a star. Tara's name means "star" in the Hindi language so it seems like she was destined to have the star-shaped mark on her side.

Tara was visiting her family when she saw an injured dolphin. She was sad for her and wished in her heart for the injured dolphin to heal.

Her star glowed and her magical powers were activated. She felt a tingle in her back and purple glitter came out of her fins.

The glitter sparkles hit the injured dolphin and she was magically healed. The dolphin swam over to Tara and said "How did you do that?"

Tara said "I wished to heal you and I'm so happy that I was able to help."

Everyone was surprised. The news of the magical healing was spread by messenger dolphins. Tara began to travel around the world to help other sea creatures in need.

One day, a messenger dolphin came to Tara and told her stories of local townspeople who were being mean to the dolphins who lived there. The townspeople were fishing too much, hurting dolphins with harpoons, and throwing litter in the water.

Tara traveled to the town and started helping all of the dolphins who were sick from the pollution with her magical powers. She went closer to the shore where the evil townspeople lived. She saw a fisherman and his wife on a boat fishing near the dolphins.

They tied a harpoon to a rope and threw it into the water at a dolphin. The dolphin got a big red cut on his flipper. They laughed as they captured the dolphin in a cage.

Tara felt sad for the captured dolphin. She was angry that the townspeople were being rude to dolphins. She used her magical powers to turn the fisherman and his wife into dolphins. They were still in their boat and got cuts on their tails from their own sharp harpoons. They jumped off the boat into the ocean.

Tara helped the injured dolphin and took him out of the cage. Happy with his cuts healed, he jumped back into the water.

Tara swam over to the fisherman and his wife who were now dolphins and said "Why are you being cruel to dolphins?" The fisherman and his wife were surprised that they had become dolphins and that a dolphin was talking to them. They felt pain in their tails because of their cuts. The fisherman said, "Why did you turn us into dolphins?"

Tara said "I turned you into dolphins so that you could experience what we feel when people are unkind to us." The fisherman and his wife were astonished.

They said "We thought dolphins had no feelings. We realize now that dolphins can get hurt by our harpoons."

Tara said "Dolphins have the same feelings that humans have. Dolphins feel the same way humans do when they get hurt. I see that you have looked within your hearts and now that you are dolphins, you see how other dolphins feel. Tell the townspeople to stop being abusive to dolphins and all sea creatures otherwise we might all die out."

The fisherman and his wife said, "We are sorry for being harsh to sea creatures, especially dolphins." Tara magically healed their cuts and transformed them back into humans. Tara said, "Remember to listen to your hearts and be kind to all people and animals."

The fisherman and his wife went to tell the townspeople to stop being mean to dolphins and sea creatures. They told everyone "We just had an adventure with dolphins! A magical dolphin turned us into dolphins and we learned that they have the same feelings that humans do and can get hurt just like we can."

The townspeople didn't believe them and laughed at the fisherman and his wife. Tara saw that the fisherman and his wife were being humiliated and the townspeople would not understand if they didn't feel the horrible pain that they were causing to dolphins.

Tara used her magical powers to turn everyone into dolphins and magically carried them into the water. The townspeople got stuck in the filthy water. They felt gross and miserable.

They begged for anyone to free them from the debris. Tara said "I will help you, once you promise to be friendly to all sea creatures." The townspeople said "We will be nice to dolphins and all sea creatures. Now we know what it is like to be dolphins swimming in polluted water."

Tara explained, "It is important to not pollute the ocean or kill dolphins and other sea life. Dolphins and other sea creatures can become extinct from the contamination."

Tara untangled them from the trash and she turned all of the townspeople back into humans again. From that time forward, nobody was mean to dolphins or sea creatures again. The townspeople found out that the filth in the water can affect them too.

Pollution makes humans and animals sick by poisoning them. Pollution can contaminate the water supply and food chain. The fisherman and his wife became the leaders of the Keep-Sea-Animals-Safe movement and the Anti-Pollution movement. They taught people to not throw trash in the ocean, use recyclable bags and be friendly to the environment.

The dolphins thanked Tara and she went back to her home. When she reached her home, her family congratulated her for helping the townspeople learn to be nice to dolphins. Everyone learned to follow the Golden Rule again.

The Golden Rule is to treat others the way you want them to treat you. Tara used her magical powers to help people bring out the good within their hearts.

The Golden Rule

Fun Facts
About Dolphins:

- Dolphins are aquatic mammals, not fish.
- There are 40 species of dolphins.
- A killer whale is also a dolphin, the largest type.
- Dolphins use echolocation to hunt for fish.
- Dolphins communicate through clicks and whistles.
- Bottlenose dolphins are the most familiar type of dolphin to humans.
- A group of dolphins is called a "school" or a "pod".
- Male dolphins are called "bulls", female dolphins are called "cows" and young dolphins are called "calves".
- Dolphins breathe through their blowholes.

About the Author:

Shreya Kumar Pradhan is a fifth-grade student who loves art and animals. This book is a result of a PTA Reflections contest entry which won 1st place at her elementary school when she was in 3rd grade. She decided to edit and illustrate the story to highlight the importance of taking care of animals, the environment and following the Golden Rule. Her school's mascot is also a dolphin. When she is not working on art, she loves playing with her three siblings, playing outside, watching movies, swimming, karate and classical Indian dance.

Made in the USA
Middletown, DE
29 April 2022

64845414R00018